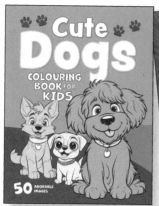

GET A FREE COLOURING BOOK

Dogs? Unicorns? Cars? Superheroes? Fashion?... The choice is yours!

Your feedback means an incredible amount to us. To say thanks for leaving us a review on Amazon we'd like to offer you a FREE COLOURING BOOK from our collection!

How to get your book

Simply leave an honest review of this colouring book on Amazon, then visit captaincolouringbook.com/claim to claim your free downloadable colouring book.

First, scan this to leave a review

Then scan this to claim your reward

www.captaincolouringbook.com

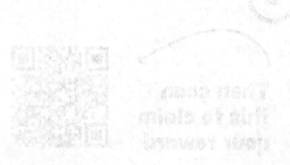

ALSO AVAILABLE FROM CAPTAIN COLOURING BOOK

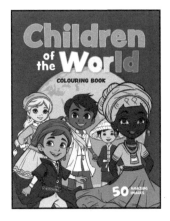

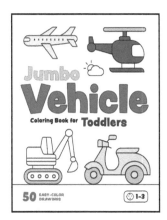

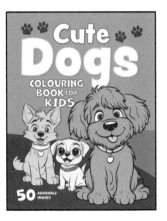

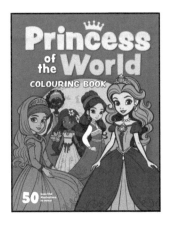

Plus many more! To see the full collection visit

www.captaincolouringbook.com

Made in United States
Troutdale, OR
12/13/2024

26493107R00060